The Adventures of
Felix & Pip

Trouble at
'Joanna Shipwreck'

by Lorraine de Kleuver

www.alysbooks.com

To Leo

The Adventures of Felix and Pip – Trouble at 'Joanna Shipwreck'

Copyright © Lorraine de Kleuver
Illustration copyright © Lorraine de Kleuver

First Edition 2017
Published by Aly's Books

www.alysbooks.com
Your Book | Our Mission

Designed by Fish Biscuit
fishbiscuitdesign.com.au

ISBN: 978-0-6480017-3-7

Felix and Pip had just arrived at Queenscliff marina on their boat, Purr-fect. After a rest they decided to walk to the shops nearby. Along the way, they stopped at Diver Dan's Dive shop.

"We should go scuba diving Pip," said Felix.

"Okay," Pip replied, "but we'll need to ask Diver Dan what we need to get."

Back on Purr-fect they changed into their diving gear. Sitting on the back steps of the boat, they prepared to go for their first dive into the water. Pip was so excited that she jumped off first.

"This is fun!" said Felix. "How about we explore around the marina a bit more?"
They both swam away from Purr-fect, but all of a sudden Pip stopped.

"Hey look!" called Pip, pointing to two small stingrays. The two young stingrays
were brother and sister. The boy was called Sandy, and his sister was called Shelley.
The four animals became instant friends.

Although Felix and Pip were new to scuba diving, Sandy and Shelley weren't. They had seen scuba divers before, so were pretty used to seeing air bubbles coming out from divers' masks.

Sandy asked Felix and Pip if they knew of places to explore.

"No, this is our first time scuba diving," said Felix.

"Well, if you like, I can show you one of my favourite places," Sandy said.

"That sounds great," said Pip.

After Sandy explained where they were to meet up, Felix and Pip returned to Purr-fect. Shelley was the only one not keen to go. She looked at her brother and quietly spoke.

"We should tell Mummy and Daddy where we're going."

"Oh, don't worry Shelley, we'll be back before they know we're gone." Shelley didn't want to disappoint her brother, so she agreed to go along.

The two young stingrays swam in the direction of St Leonard's, where they planned to meet up with their new friends.

Along the way, they swam over wide sandy grasslands, and saw lots of different types of sea animals.

Meanwhile, Felix and Pip were feeling hungry, so they decided to visit a kiosk at St Leonard's.

When they got there, Felix found a place for them to sit, while Pip went inside to buy a large milkshake. With two straws, they shared their banana milkshake, before sailing back to meet Sandy and Shelley.

The four friends met up, deep under water, and Sandy showed Felix and Pip his favourite place.

"It's a shipwreck," he told them. "It's called Joanna, and has loads of heavy broken bags. I've been told there's treasure there if you dig below the bags."

They swam around exploring the wreck.

"Hey look, I found a silver spoon deep in the sand," Pip called out. Felix, Sandy and Shelley were excited about what she had found.

As Felix and Pip searched further around the wreck, Shelley quietly pulled her brother aside.

"Remember, you said that we wouldn't be long."

"Oh Shelley, we won't be long, and look, our new friends are finding more things!"

Pip was digging in the sand, and found another treasure – a beautiful blue and white cup. Shelley swam over to her, using her tail to help pick it up.

"Oh Pip, what a pretty cup you found," she said.

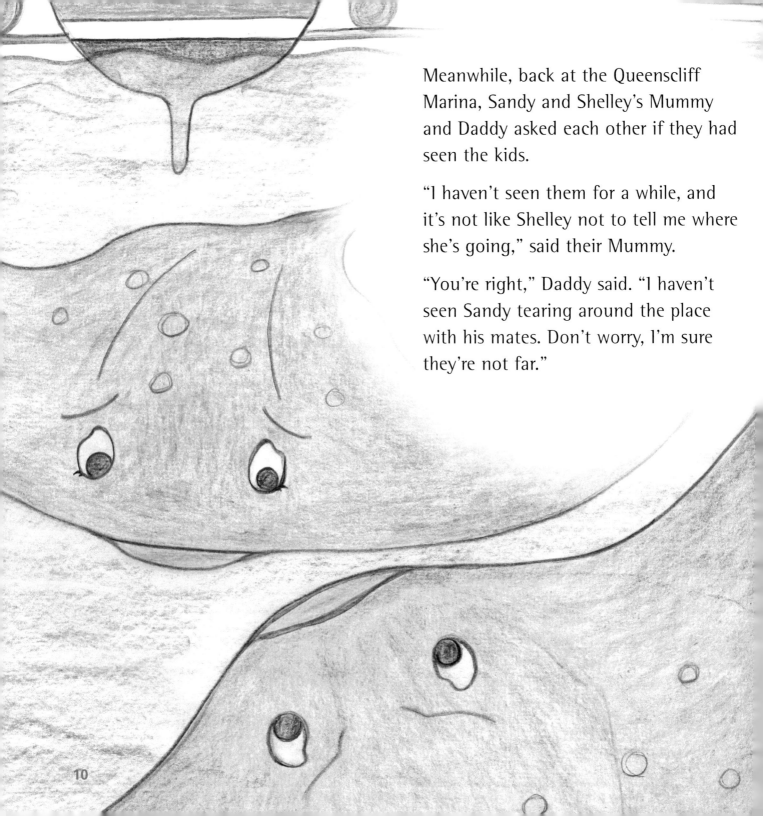

Meanwhile, back at the Queenscliff Marina, Sandy and Shelley's Mummy and Daddy asked each other if they had seen the kids.

"I haven't seen them for a while, and it's not like Shelley not to tell me where she's going," said their Mummy.

"You're right," Daddy said. "I haven't seen Sandy tearing around the place with his mates. Don't worry, I'm sure they're not far."

All the same though, Daddy asked some of his mates to help him search for Sandy and Shelley, just to make sure.

They searched under the pier, and other nooks and crannies where their father knew his kids liked to swim and play, but they still couldn't find them. Daddy began to get really worried.

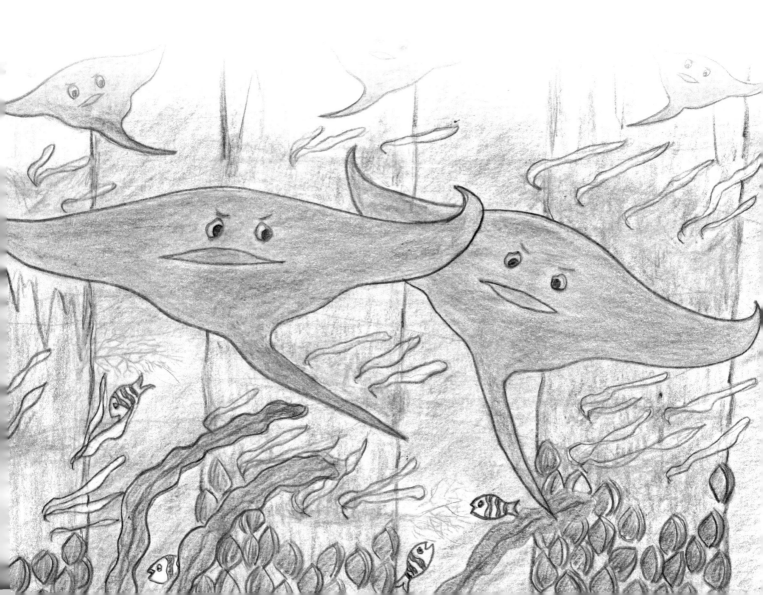

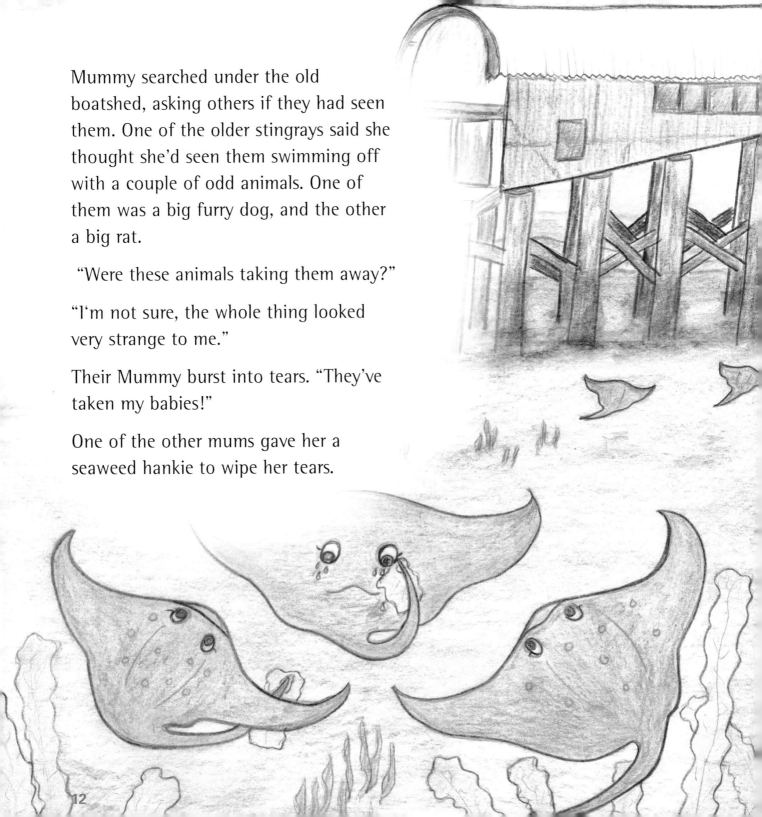

Mummy searched under the old boatshed, asking others if they had seen them. One of the older stingrays said she thought she'd seen them swimming off with a couple of odd animals. One of them was a big furry dog, and the other a big rat.

"Were these animals taking them away?"

"I'm not sure, the whole thing looked very strange to me."

Their Mummy burst into tears. "They've taken my babies!"

One of the other mums gave her a seaweed hankie to wipe her tears.

While everyone back at the marina was worried and concerned for Sandy and Shelley, they were happily playing around with their new friends Felix and Pip.

The stingrays used their tails to help move the sand away for Felix and Pip, and working together they found another beautiful blue and white plate. "Wow," they all said. The four friends were so happy with their new find.

Back at the marina, Sandy and Shelley's Mummy told their Daddy that they had been seen with a couple of strange animals.

"It's all very worrying," said Daddy. "Our kids usually introduce us to their new friends, and say where they live. It's not like them at all. I'm going to tell the Stingray Police that they're missing."

Mummy burst into tears again.

When Daddy got to the Stingray Police station, he explained what had happened and gave them a photo of Sandy and Shelley.

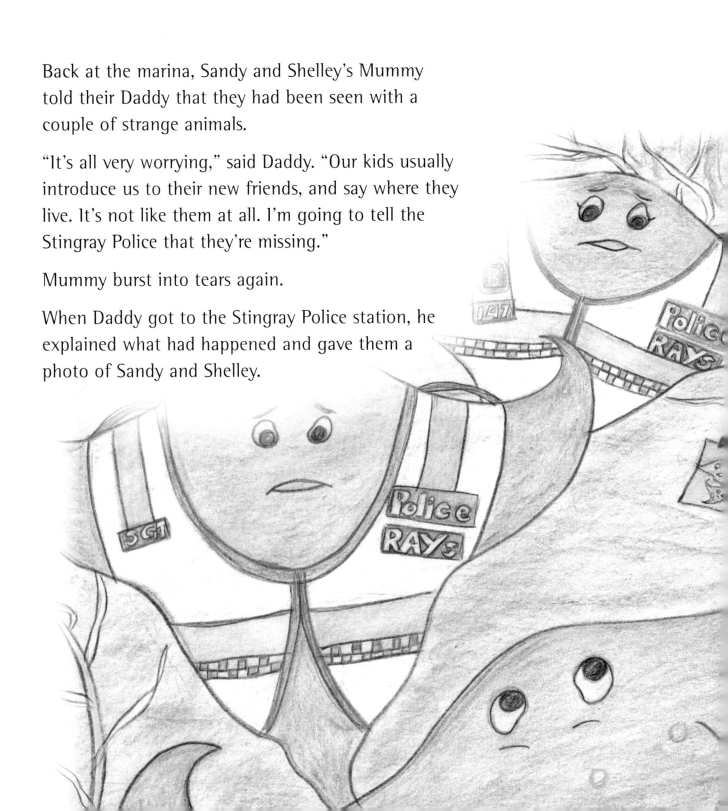

Back at the Joanna shipwreck, the four friends were having so much fun that they lost track of time. It wasn't until Felix decided to look at his watch that he realised how late it was.

"Oh no!" he gasped. Pip saw a lot of bubbles coming out of Felix's mask, so she swam over to him.

"What's up Felix?" she asked. Felix showed Pip his watch, which showed only an hour of oxygen left in his tank. Pip was shocked.

Felix and Pip explained that they couldn't stay much longer, and the four friends agreed that they should go soon, but not just yet – they were still having so much fun.

As they played, the Queenscliff Stingray Police (fondly known as the Police Rays), were searching for the two young stingrays. Hundreds of Police Rays swam out in different directions, all carrying searchlights to help them see into dark places.

One of the search groups was lead by Sergeant Sally. She was a Mummy herself, and was determined to try and find the two little stingrays.

They searched towards St Leonard's, thinking the worst, but hoping for the best.

Felix became aware of a large dark shape coming towards them. "Look!" he called out, pointing towards the large shape. "I think it's a monster with lots of lights coming towards us." They looked towards it, not sure what to do.

Before they could swim away, the large dark shape was above them. Sandy realised it was the Police Rays, shining lights down on them, and he sensed that he may be in trouble.

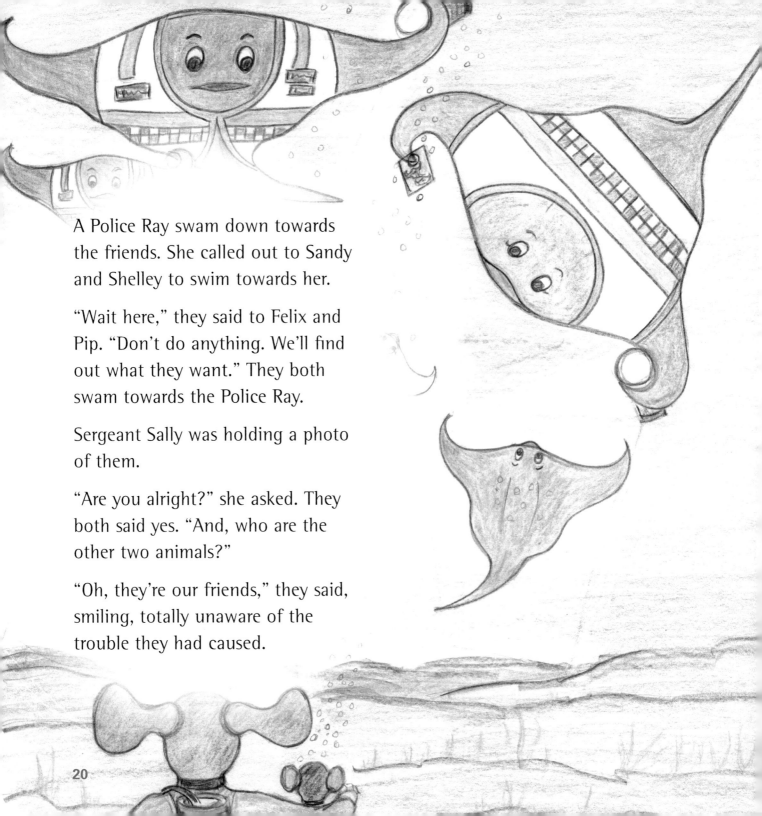

A Police Ray swam down towards the friends. She called out to Sandy and Shelley to swim towards her.

"Wait here," they said to Felix and Pip. "Don't do anything. We'll find out what they want." They both swam towards the Police Ray.

Sergeant Sally was holding a photo of them.

"Are you alright?" she asked. They both said yes. "And, who are the other two animals?"

"Oh, they're our friends," they said, smiling, totally unaware of the trouble they had caused.

"Well you two, we better get you home because your parents are really worried," Sergeant Sally said.

"Can we say goodbye to our friends?" Sandy asked.

"Of course, but don't be long!"

Sandy and Shelley swam down to their friends, who were still too scared to move. Sandy told them why the Police Rays were there. "Well, I guess you won't be making that mistake again," said Felix with smile.

"No he won't." said Shelley firmly.

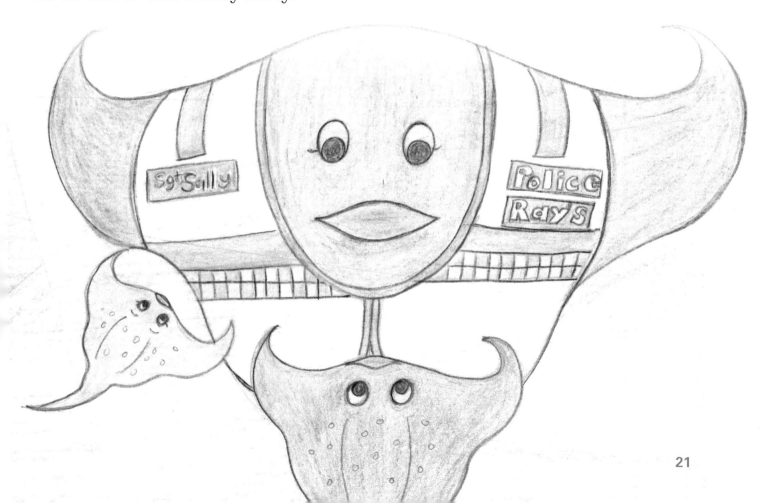

Sandy and Shelley were escorted home by Sergeant Sally and the Police Rays, and reminded of the importance of letting their Mummy and Daddy know where they were going.

"At all times," said Sergeant Sally, pointing at them.

As soon as they reached Queenscliff their Mummy and Daddy rushed out towards them. When Sandy and Shelley saw them they raced towards them calling out, "Mummy! Daddy!"

"Oh, we're so happy that you're both safe," said their Mummy.

Always
Tell
Mum & Dad
Where You Are
Going –
and Who You
are with.

The following day at Sea School, Sergeant Sally was there to greet them. They knew they were going to get another lesson that they would never, ever forget.

With a thick red pen, Sergeant Sally wrote on the school board the following message: Always tell your Mum and Dad where you are going – and who you are with.

"I want you all to remember this message!"

After Felix and Pip sailed Purr-fect back to the Queenscliff marina, they decided to take a walk to the viewing tower.

"I guess our new friends have learned a very important lesson," said Felix.

"Yes, their Mummy and Daddy were very worried. I guess, it's important for us as well," Pip said. "We should always let Coast Radio Melbourne know where we are when we sail out on Purr-fect."

Felix nodded. "It's really just letting people know we're safe, so that they don't worry."

Author's Notes

Did you know that Port Phillip Bay – is not a Bay!

Well, it's actually a 'Port,' and is officially referred to as Port Phillip. Unofficially though, it's fondly called Port Phillip Bay – or – the Bay.

There are 17 Bays in Port Phillip, and they are:-

Altona Bay, Balcons Bay, Beaumaris Bay, Camerons Bight, Capel Sound, Collins Bay, Corio Bay, Dromana Bay, Hobson Bay, Limeburners Bay, Lonsdale Bay, Nepean Bay, Stingaree Bay, Sullivans Bay, Swan Bay, Watkins Bay, Weeroona Bay.

The Smooth Stingray

The illustrations in this story are based on the Smooth Stingrays that visit the Queenscliff Marina. They are one of the largest stingrays in the world. And when you see them at the marina, you will see for yourself how LARGE they really are.

Special Note

It goes without saying that to produce a book; in this case a children's story, there's always more than one person that get's it off-and-running. In my case, I have many people; first and foremost, my husband and best buddy Co, for his unstinting patience and support, then of course my publisher and her team, website support, friends and family support – and of course – the big wide world that is Facebook. The support from Facebook followers with the 'Journey' has been wonderful – Lots of Likes and Loves to you all.

The Author would like to acknowledge Annie Muir, Heritage Curator, Heritage Victoria, for her assistance in making this book a better story. Also to Les Irving-Dusting, for his bottomless knowledge on the 'Joanna,' Wendy Parker, Administration Manager, and Robert Styles, all respectively from the Queenscliff Maritime Museum, for their valuable assistance.

The Adventures of
Felix & Pip

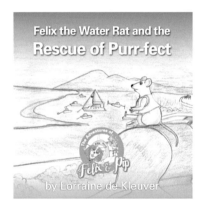

Felix the Water Rat and the
Rescue of Purr-fect

by Lorraine de Kleuver

**The Missing
Baby Dragon**

by Lorraine de Kleuver

**Trouble at
'Joanna
Shipwreck'**

by Lorraine de Kleuver